Plague!

Stories linking with the History
National Curriculum Key Stage 2

First published in 1999 by Franklin Watts
96 Leonard Street, London EC2A 4XD

Editor: Sarah Snashall
Designer: Jason Anscomb
Consultant: Dr Anne Millard, BA Hons, Dip Ed, PhD

A CIP catalogue record for this book
is available from the British Library.

ISBN   0 7496 3365 4 (hbk)
       0 7496 3556 8 (pbk)

Dewey Classification 942.05

Printed in Great Britain

Plague!

**Written and illustrated by
George Buchanan**

W

FRANKLIN WATTS

NEW YORK • LONDON • SYDNEY

1
Strangers

A young girl clutches her cloak tightly and picks her way across the pebbles. She steps between the bleached bones and fish heads, snippets of tarry rope and oddments of rusty iron, towards the luggers pulled up on the beach.

She waits in the shelter of a black boat and watches the sparkling sea. There are fishing boats in the distance, racing for the shore. She is watching one, black-hulled and black-sailed, which is thrashing towards the beach. It is bringing a secret visitor to England.

"Well, it'll be fish today, for a religious little Miss like you, won't it, Miss Sarah?"

Obidiah Adams leans over the side of his boat, and looks down at her. "Did you know, Miss, I've been made a watchman? I'll do my civic duty for a year, and glad to, but guess who's in charge of my watch. It's Mr Misery himself, Ezekiel Killjoy Watkins. He's hot after Catholics, you know. First thing he said was for us to report any Catholics, and any strangers, too. Now why would he want that, do you think?"

She looks up. She knows that it is illegal to hide Catholics, or to worship as a Catholic. Her secret visitor is a Catholic priest. Would her friend Obidiah give her away?

"So, does Master Adams think that eating fish on a Friday makes me a Catholic? And what will you be eating today?" she laughs, "Fresh herring washed down with the best smuggled brandy, I don't doubt?"

Just beyond the breakers, they

watch the black lugger sail along the shore.
Picking a wave, it suddenly turns, heels and,
riding its crest, is swept up the
beach in a thunder of spray.

"But, tell me Obidiah,"
she asks, "why are
they are pulling down
the pest house?
They were ripping
off the roof
when I
went past."

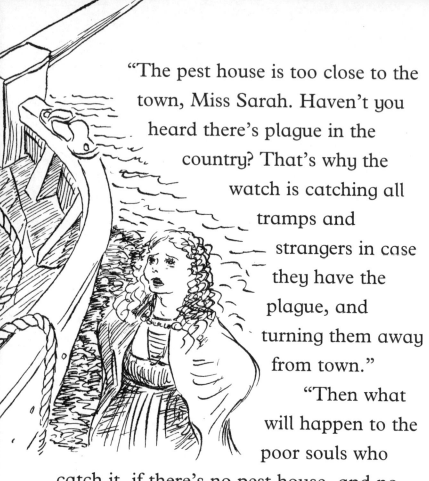

"The pest house is too close to the town, Miss Sarah. Haven't you heard there's plague in the country? That's why the watch is catching all tramps and strangers in case they have the plague, and turning them away from town."

"Then what will happen to the poor souls who catch it, if there's no pest house, and no one to care for them?" she asks.

"We don't have the plague here, Miss."

"But we will, Obidiah, and then what will happen?"

"We are to lock them up in their houses,

10

Miss, and let them out at night only."

She stares up at him. "Then all the household will perish, Obidiah. How can you do that?"

"It's our orders, Miss Sarah. Look, they have something for you." He nods at the black lugger being pulled up the beach. "You'd better go."

★★★

Sarah walks across. A horse is straining at a capstan, heaving the boat further up the beach. Men are dropping heavy planks onto the stones for the boat to slide on.

As she steps nearer, a figure, huddled in oilskins, climbs down from the deck. A fisherman holds his arm.

"Quickly, Miss, take him away," he mutters. "It's Father Robert. Be quick!"

The man staggers beside her.

"Are you ill, Father?" she asks.

"Only seasickness, bless you. I'll be better soon."

As they pass, Obidiah meets them. "A portion of turbot for you, Miss."

He hands her a slippery parcel. A great fin, two spans wide, pokes out from the end.

"It will feed your family, and your guest," he adds, looking at the stranger.

"My best respects to your parents, Miss Sarah, and to you, Father," he bows awkwardly. "Not that I've seen you," he says, meaningfully, "as I'm officially in the watch now, you understand."

2
The light

They leave the beach. The door of the pest house is open, and men are carrying chests and boxes out to a cart. Others stand in the roof trusses, knocking the beams apart with wooden mallets. The used thatch is raked into a heap, and bedding and old clothes are thrown onto the pile.

"They are moving the pest house, and are going to rebuild it outside the town walls," whispers Sarah. "We have the plague in the country round us. I hope they are in time."

"What is the sort of plague that you are frightened of, child?" he asks. "Is it the smallpox, or the fever, or is it the black plague

that we have in France at the moment?"

"Father, I don't know. Some say it is the pox, others the black death, but we have no true accounts. I am sure I wouldn't know the difference anyway."

"You would, child, believe me," he mutters.

★★★

The sun is setting over the sea as they enter the narrow streets of the town. The church bells are tolling, a signal to the farmers to bring in their pigs and their cattle. They walk in the shadows at the edges of the lanes, Sarah guiding the stranger.

They turn off the street, and climb some steps crammed between tall wooden houses. It is dark in the narrow alley.

Pigs and goats shamble by as they

wait in a doorway. Some cows sway past, driven by a young boy. He sees them and dodges across.

"Hello, Miss Sarah. Good evening, Sir! Would you be wanting the light tonight, Miss?" he adds in a whisper.

"Oh James! If you can it would be splendid."

"I will do anything for you, Miss, you knows that!" he stammers awkwardly. Then he adds, "Do you know,

Master Watkins and part of the watch is out already, looking for strangers? And it's not even dark yet!"

"Where are they?"

"They are watching the land gate, and the sergeant and two men are watching the crowds crossing the bridge. You'd better be careful, Miss."

They move off up the alley, and turn right into a maze of narrow passages, stairways and tunnels. They cross a bustling street, stepping around the animals rooting in the rubbish, and avoiding the

puddles and piles of dung and filth heaped in the centre. Then they dive back into the darkness of the alleys and passageways.

Their path takes them to the east and upwards. Soon they can look over the roofs of the crowded buildings, to the harbour and the fishing boats drawn up the beach. They stop as they reach a tall, wooden house, crammed between two lanes.

By the heavy oak door is a wooden plate with 'Peter Mose, Apothecary and Montebank' painted on it.

"You must stay with us for a while, Father," says Sarah. "Later we will help you to travel to Tonbridge."

The evening sun glints off the diamond-paned windows, and off the red tiled roof. Behind it, a string of cottages leads to the cliff itself, glowing bright pink in the evening light.

They look down. By the shore they see

the flickering of the blazing thatch. A pillar of thick smoke climbs over the valley.

"In the Low Countries, I hear they are burning the bodies," mutters the priest, as Sarah pulls open the front door. "Let us hope we are spared."

3

Plague

Father Robert is given a small room of his
own. He climbs up the winding oak stairs
to the attic, where the servants live. A chest
is dragged sideways, and a panel in the
plasterwork is pushed back. Inside, between
the roof tiles and the servants' room is a

long narrow chamber, and in it stands
a bed, a stool and a chest. There are
no windows.

Downstairs, Sarah knocks on the door
of her father's study. She goes in. He sits
at a table reading a heavy leather-bound
book, and makes notes with a stick of
charcoal on a scrap of paper. He is
dressed for outdoors.

"Are you going out, Father?" Sarah

asks. "I have the new priest upstairs. Shall I call him down to meet you?"

"There is no time, my dear, just make sure he is comfortable. Please ask if he will kindly hold Mass for us tonight. I have more sickness than I can cope with. It's the summer heat. Soon a priest will be more use than a mere apothecary and montebank."

"I saw James. He will light the candle when it is safe."

"Then we will await his signal."

★★★

For a week, Father Robert lives in the house. In the evenings a steady trickle of men and women secretly enter the house, to make their confession and to hear Mass. Each night a solitary candle flickers in an upstairs window of the Mayor's mansion across the valley. It is James's signal: they are safe for the moment, and will not be disturbed.

Now, by day and by night, people come

to the front door and knock. They appeal
for help. There is sickness and the fear of
plague. Already there is talk that the plague
has struck in the parish of St. Bennets.
Sarah and her mother spend all day in the
surgery, weighing and wrapping small
bundles of crushed frankincense and pitch,
which Peter Mose takes with him on his
visits. It is a disinfectant which
is burnt in the rooms of
the sick.

Then, one day, Peter comes back tired and shaking. He has encountered his first case of plague: a small, terrified child, covered with boils, and with black swellings in his armpits that ooze foul-smelling pus. The poor child and his frightened family huddle together for comfort while Peter makes his report to the mayor. The watch is called, the door of their shabby hut is locked shut and someone scratches 'Lord have mercy' across it.

The next day, twenty more cases are reported. Panic spreads through the town.

Peter Mose never rests. All day he attends the sick. On his way, mothers and fathers plead with him for help. On his weary route home, panic-stricken husbands and wives shout at him. They offer gold, cattle, barrels of brandy – anything and everything in exchange for help. Always, he goes to their aid.

Entering the sickroom he smells the odour of rotting flesh. He dispenses disinfectant, cleans the patients, cools them with wet cloths, and promises to return. He expresses hope, but knows they are doomed. Six days at the most they have to live.

Wearily he climbs upstairs to the servants' room, and knocks on the secret door. "Father," he whispers, "I have patients who are dying. Some are Catholics and are calling for a priest. Will you see them?"

Father Robert opens the door. "I have been waiting for this," he answers. "You must guide me."

3
Night

A wild banging on the front door stops
them in the hall. Peter hustles the priest
out of sight. The maid opens the door,
and a young woman carrying a tiny baby
rushes in.

"Take her," she pleads, "Please take her.

The watch has ordered her to be locked up with her family. But they have three cases of plague already, and she will surely die."

"I know this child," says Peter, "it's little Molly Russell. I didn't know her family were stricken. Take her into the kitchen, Katherine, and give her food and some new blankets. Burn these filthy ones. We shall care for her. But now you must leave, I have urgent visits to make."

More heavy knocking. Two men report a new outbreak in Ropewalk Alley. Can he come?

Peter calls Sarah. She runs in from the front

room. "Sarah, will you please take Father Robert to the Isles' house and then to the Morrisons'? They have called for the last rites. You know where they live don't you? I must go with these two men."

"I will, Father, but did you know that James has been signalling from the Mayor's house. Three candles – it means the watch is looking for our priest! It's Watkins again, he has spies everywhere!"

"Then hurry away, child," says her father, "and they will find no-one at home."

***

The night is black, but the streets are alive with people and animals. Only the sick and a few brave souls venture out at night. Abandoned animals forage for food in the rubbish, rats turn and scuttle away. Three stray cows, looking for comfort and fodder, turn and follow Sarah and Father Robert as they head for the poor parish of St. Bennets. From the windows they can hear the crying and moaning of desperate people. They step round bodies that lie sleeping or dead in the path. Only the alehouses are ablaze with light and noise, drunkenness, and fighting.

"It is just as in France," mutters the priest. "People have given up hope."

"I haven't given up hope, Father," Sarah protests, "and neither has my father. We will never give up!"

"God bless you, my dear," he mutters. "You are a braver soul than I am."

They step aside to let a cart pass by. Hooded men toss the dead bodies onto the cart and move on.

They reach a small tumbledown cottage. The door is dragged open and

they squeeze inside. An old lady, bowing and thanking them as she goes, ushers them into a small chamber. The priest pulls off his hood and stoops over an old man lying on a straw mattress. He mutters a prayer, and makes the sign of the cross. The man's face is stretched in despair, but his eyes follow the priest and he looks up when the service is finished.

"Thank you, Father," he croaks, "I never

thought I'd see a priest again."

The old lady shows them out, pressing copper coins into the priest's hands, and a rough shawl into Sarah's. "It is an old shawl and a beautiful one, Miss Sarah, and I would be proud for you to have it," she says. "Now my husband can die in peace."

"But Mrs Isles, we never knew you were Catholics," whispers Sarah.

"We don't change our faith at the word of a mayor or a Queen, child," she mutters. "There are many who think likewise in this parish."

4

The watch

They hustle back through squalid lanes
and passageways, dart over the footbridge
and dive once more into the dark lanes and
alleyways of the East Hill. They skirt round
the foraging animals, and hasten past the
wandering sick who stagger and slip

awkwardly in the muck. A pack of scruffy
dogs follows them, barking. Knowing the
dogs will attract attention, Sarah
takes a stick and beats
them off.

As they climb, they notice grass
sprouting between the cobbles and growing
on the piles of refuse which block the central
drain. The whole town seems to be dying.

There is shouting behind them.
Looking back, Sarah sees a lantern,
swinging on the end of a long staff.

"Quick Father!" she pants. "We are
being followed."

Holding hands, they scramble up a narrow string of steps and disappear into a damp and smelly alley.

She hammers on a broken door, and pushes inside. By the candlelight they see a figure kneeling by a low bed, crying quietly. Three small children, stiff and white, lie across the mattress. In the bed there is a man. His large lifeless hands droop over the blanket.

Father Robert lifts Mrs Morrison to her feet, leans over each child, and makes the sign of the cross.

"Father," she sobs, "he could take no more. Both

boys were buried last week, and when little Annie and the twins died, not an hour ago, he killed himself! I tried to stop him, and now he won't even have a Christian burial!"

"You poor struggling people," mutters Father Robert. "Let your man be buried with the rest of your family. Surely they are all victims of the plague? Daily I shall say prayers for his soul."

There is a clattering and shouting outside. Sarah peers round the door. Ezekiel Watkins and three big men are

blocking the alley and searching the houses. Obidiah is holding the lamp. He sees her, opens his mouth to cry out, then drops the lamp, plunging the alley into darkness.

"Quickly, Father," she whispers. "Blow out the candle and they won't see us. We must flee!"

They slide out of the door, and keeping in the shadows, slip into a side passage and run.

Someone small and fast is chasing them. They step into a doorway and a

thin young man flashes past.

"James!" she calls out. He stops.

"Oh, Miss Sarah! I have been trying to warn you! You must take the priest and get him out of town. There's not a minute to lose. The watch will be on us!"

He leads them away through strange narrow passages, leaving their pursuers far behind. Suddenly they stumble out into the steep cobbled lane opposite Sarah's house.

"It's Watkins, he knows about the priest. He'll be here in a minute to search your house. Send Father Robert away, Miss, for your own safety. Collect his things, and take him away from here!"

She flashes a smile "Thank you James!" she says, and pulls the breathless priest indoors.

5
The tunnel

Up the stairs into the attic they rush. She waits while Father Robert drops his belongings into a soft leather bag. Then she leads him to the kitchen, and into the dairy. Men are beating on the front door. She opens a large cupboard.

"Follow me, Father!"

She pushes the shelves aside. Then she heaves at the back panels, until they slide slowly sideways.

"Come through," she whispers. They can hear the tramp of feet and shouting as the watch clamber the stairs to the attic.

She draws back the shelves, and together they push the panelling shut.

"Hold my hand," she whispers. "I know the way."

They are in a tunnel. Father Robert
can feel the sandy floor and sandy walls.
Sarah opens a small door into a cellar.
They must be next door. They cross the

cellar and squeeze
through a rough iron
door and begin to
climb. The walls are
warm, but clean. They
must be climbing up
the outside of a large
brick chimney. She
stops to open a
wooden hatch, and
they step through.

Now they are in
a narrow loft. They
creep beneath the
rafters, and struggle
under low doorways.

"All these roofs are connected," she says. "Smugglers use them now, but they were once escape routes for when the French attacked."

They stop at a solid wooden door in a brick wall. She turns the key and they step out into fresh air. A gentle breeze brushes their faces as they look over the roofs of the little town. It is a beautiful night.

Sarah shuts the door quietly, and together they cross the springy turf. There is not a soul in sight.

6
The glen

A short walk brings them to the edge of a steep valley. Sarah leads Father Robert down a narrow pathway and stops by a thick holly bush.

"Wriggle through here," she says, and lies down and crawls across the sharp crackly leaves. Father Robert follows.

They can stand up behind the bush. In the darkness he stretches out his hand behind him. No cliff, nothing.

"Come back here," she whispers.

He stumbles back into a large cave.

"There is a bed," she whispers, "and there is water and a cup." She holds his hand and guides it to the bed, and then to the tankard of water.

Breathing heavily, Father Robert lowers himself onto the bed.

"Water, dear. I feel strangely hot," he mutters, taking a long drink, and shivering. "Thank you, Sarah. You must go now."

"Tomorrow evening, James will bring food. Goodnight to you, Father," she says and, drawing the shawl round her, is gone.

★★★

"Father, can you hear me?" James leans across the bed, and looks down on the priest. He is huddled on the bed, shuddering with cold, yet his face is burning red, and covered with perspiration.

He opens his eyes.

"Who is it?" he asks. He struggles to sit up, but collapses, coughing.

There is blood on his lips, and on the edge of the mattress. He draws his hand across his mouth, then stares at it. It is streaked with blood.

"Water," he mutters. "Keep away, child, I am full of plague. Bring water, and leave me."

"I will fetch Peter Mose."

***

Three figures race across the grass and stumble into the glen.

"Show me where he is hidden."

They scrabble under the holly bush. Peter lights his lantern.

All is still. There is a body on the bed.
One hand grips a small black book.
A crucifix and a chalice are toppled on
the floor.

Peter leans over the dead priest.

"So quick," he mutters. "No bruising,
no swellings, but the same smell of
mortification and decay."

They hear voices. Someone shouts,
"Come on out, Peter Mose! And the priest!
We have you!"

"It's the watch!" whispers James.

"Then come in, Watchmen! The priest is waiting for you," Peter shouts.

Three men clatter into the cave shouting, "Stand back! Don't move! Drop your weapons!"

They stare at the bed muttering, and shuffle awkwardly.

Sarah steps forwards.

"Obidiah, Jason, Berridge! Here is your brave, hunted priest. He went without sticks and truncheons into the houses of the sick to give comfort.

Take him now," she shouts, "he has been serving a different master, and a greater one."

Obidiah looks down at her. "We can't match you in words or goodness, Miss Sarah. We'll go, and report nothing."

Peter looks up from the priest. "Report

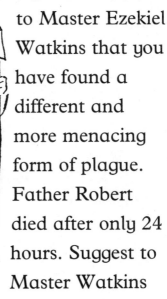

to Master Ezekiel Watkins that you have found a different and more menacing form of plague. Father Robert died after only 24 hours. Suggest to Master Watkins that he enforces the strictest isolation of the sick. Perhaps Master Watkins should spend his energies in combating the plague, and if you have the courage, suggest that he stops hounding those of us who are giving comfort and help to the dying. This is a new form of the plague, tell him. It is quick and deadly. No one is safe. Who knows where this will end?"

Notes

Black Death

Bubonic plague appeared in Europe in 1347. It was called the Black Death and killed almost 30 per cent of the population of Europe between  1347 and 1350. In some areas 90 per cent of the population died. From that time onwards, Europe suffered frequent outbreaks of the plague.

People did not know how the disease spread. In 1348, professors of medicine at the University of Paris believed the plague was caused by the position of the stars and planets.

Tudor plague

A major outbreak of plague took place in Europe in the 16th century, when our story is set. People still didn't know what caused the plague, but they did

understand that plague could be passed from person to person. During a plague epidemic, laws prevented people from moving around spreading the plague. In a small outbreak, plague victims could be isolated in pest houses. In an epidemic, these became full and sufferers were confined in their homes.

Cleaning up

By the end of the 16th century, people began to realise that the conditions in the towns allowed plague to flourish – household waste (including excrement) was dumped in the streets, and animals were allowed to roam freely. Rules were introduced to control where animals were kept and how waste was disposed of.

Fleas and rats

In 1894, Alexandre Yersin discovered that the bubonic plague is a bacteria that lives in the stomach of the flea, and in the bloodstream of its host, the black rat or the brown sewer rat. The plague bacteria is passed to humans when a person is bitten by a flea carrying the disease. In a few days, the infected person develops a fever and boils that can be as large as an egg or an orange.

Once an epidemic of bubonic plague has lasted some time, pneumonic, and then septicaemic plague may develop. These are much more violent forms of the disease and victims often die before boils can develop. The bacteria of these forms of plague can be passed on when an infected person coughs or sneezes.

Catholics and Protestants

This story is set during the reign of Elizabeth I (1558–1603). England was a Protestant country at this time and everyone was expected to follow the Protestant faith. Previously, England had been a Catholic country under the reign of Mary (1553–1558). People then had been forced to follow the Roman Catholic faith and Protestants were persecuted.

QUEEN ELIZABETH I

During the reign of Elizabeth I, the government introduced measures to stamp out the Catholic faith. Catholics had to practise their religion secretly.

Many people thought that when Elizabeth died, England would become a Roman Catholic country again. Catholic priests from France travelled around England preaching the Catholic faith.

In Tudor England, many people saw the plague as a punishment from God. Secretly, Catholics blamed the Protestant faith for the troubles.

Sparks: Historical Adventures

ANCIENT GREECE
The Great Horse of Troy – The Trojan War
0 7496 3369 7 (hbk)   0 7496 3538 X (pbk)
The Winner's Wreath – Ancient Greek Olympics
0 7496 3368 9 (hbk)   0 7496 3555 X (pbk)

INVADERS AND SETTLERS
Boudicca Strikes Back – The Romans in Britain
0 7496 3366 2 (hbk)   0 7496 3546 0 (pbk)
Viking Raiders – A Norse Attack
0 7496 3089 2 (hbk)   0 7496 3457 X (pbk)
Erik's New Home – A Viking Town
0 7496 3367 0 (hbk)   0 7496 3552 5 (pbk)
TALES OF THE ROWDY ROMANS
The Great Necklace Hunt
0 7496 2221 0 (hbk)   0 7496 2628 3 (pbk)
The Lost Legionary
0 7496 2222 9 (hbk)   0 7496 2629 1 (pbk)
The Guard Dog Geese
0 7496 2331 4 (hbk)   0 7496 2630 5 (pbk)
A Runaway Donkey
0 7496 2332 2 (hbk)   0 7496 2631 3 (pbk)

TUDORS AND STUARTS
Captain Drake's Orders – The Armada
0 7496 2556 2 (hbk)   0 7496 3121 X (pbk)
London's Burning – The Great Fire of London
0 7496 2557 0 (hbk)   0 7496 3122 8 (pbk)
Mystery at the Globe – Shakespeare's Theatre
0 7496 3096 5 (hbk)   0 7496 3449 9 (pbk)
Plague! – A Tudor Epidemic
0 7496 3365 4 (hbk)   0 7496 3556 8 (pbk)
Stranger in the Glen – Rob Roy
0 7496 2586 4 (hbk)   0 7496 3123 6 (pbk)
A Dream of Danger – The Massacre of Glencoe
0 7496 2587 2 (hbk)   0 7496 3124 4 (pbk)
A Queen's Promise – Mary Queen of Scots
0 7496 2589 9 (hbk)   0 7496 3125 2 (pbk)
Over the Sea to Skye – Bonnie Prince Charlie
0 7496 2588 0 (hbk)   0 7496 3126 0 (pbk)
TALES OF A TUDOR TEARAWAY
A Pig Called Henry
0 7496 2204 4 (hbk)   0 7496 2625 9 (pbk)
A Horse Called Deathblow
0 7496 2205 9 (hbk)   0 7496 2624 0 (pbk)
Dancing for Captain Drake
0 7496 2234 2 (hbk)   0 7496 2626 7 (pbk)
Birthdays are a Serious Business
0 7496 2235 0 (hbk)   0 7496 2627 5 (pbk)

VICTORIAN ERA
The Runaway Slave – The British Slave Trade
0 7496 3093 0 (hbk)   0 7496 3456 1 (pbk)
The Sewer Sleuth – Victorian Cholera
0 7496 2590 2 (hbk)   0 7496 3128 7 (pbk)
Convict! – Criminals Sent to Australia
0 7496 2591 0 (hbk)   0 7496 3129 5 (pbk)
An Indian Adventure – Victorian India
0 7496 3090 6 (hbk)   0 7496 3451 0 (pbk)
Farewell to Ireland – Emigration to America
0 7496 3094 9 (hbk)   0 7496 3448 0 (pbk)

The Great Hunger – Famine in Ireland
0 7496 3095 7 (hbk)   0 7496 3447 2 (pbk)
Fire Down the Pit – A Welsh Mining Disaster
0 7496 3091 4 (hbk)   0 7496 3450 2 (pbk)
Tunnel Rescue – The Great Western Railway
0 7496 3353 0 (hbk)   0 7496 3537 1 (pbk)
Kidnap on the Canal – Victorian Waterways
0 7496 3352 2 (hbk)   0 7496 3540 1 (pbk)
Dr. Barnardo's Boys – Victorian Charity
0 7496 3358 1 (hbk)   0 7496 3541 X (pbk)
The Iron Ship – Brunel's Great Britain
0 7496 3355 7 (hbk)   0 7496 3543 6 (pbk)
Bodies for Sale – Victorian Tomb-Robbers
0 7496 3364 6 (hbk)   0 7496 3539 8 (pbk)
Penny Post Boy – The Victorian Postal Service
0 7496 3362 X (hbk)   0 7496 3544 4 (pbk)
The Canal Diggers – The Manchester Ship Canal
0 7496 3356 5 (hbk)   0 7496 3545 2 (pbk)
The Tay Bridge Tragedy – A Victorian Disaster
0 7496 3354 9 (hbk)   0 7496 3547 9 (pbk)
Stop, Thief! – The Victorian Police
0 7496 3359 X (hbk)   0 7496 3548 7 (pbk)
A School – for Girls! – Victorian Schools
0 7496 3360 3 (hbk)   0 7496 3549 5 (pbk)
Chimney Charlie – Victorian Chimney Sweeps
0 7496 3351 4 (hbk)   0 7496 3551 7 (pbk)
Down the Drain – Victorian Sewers
0 7496 3357 3 (hbk)   0 7496 3550 9 (pbk)
The Ideal Home – A Victorian New Town
0 7496 3361 1 (hbk)   0 7496 3553 3 (pbk)
Stage Struck – Victorian Music Hall
0 7496 3363 8 (hbk)   0 7496 3554 1 (pbk)
TRAVELS OF A YOUNG VICTORIAN
The Golden Key
0 7496 2360 8 (hbk)   0 7496 2632 1 (pbk)
Poppy's Big Push
0 7496 2361 6 (hbk)   0 7496 2633 X (pbk)
Poppy's Secret
0 7496 2374 8 (hbk)   0 7496 2634 8 (pbk)
The Lost Treasure
0 7496 2375 6 (hbk)   0 7496 2635 6 (pbk)

20th-CENTURY HISTORY
Fight for the Vote – The Suffragettes
0 7496 3092 2 (hbk)   0 7496 3452 9 (pbk)
The Road to London – The Jarrow March
0 7496 2609 7 (hbk)   0 7496 3132 5 (pbk)
The Sandbag Secret – The Blitz
0 7496 2608 9 (hbk)   0 7496 3133 3 (pbk)
Sid's War – Evacuation
0 7496 3209 7 (hbk)   0 7496 3445 6 (pbk)
D-Day! – Wartime Adventure
0 7496 3208 9 (hbk)   0 7496 3446 4 (pbk)
The Prisoner – A Prisoner of War
0 7496 3212 7 (hbk)   0 7496 3455 3 (pbk)
Escape from Germany – Wartime Refugees
0 7496 3211 9 (hbk)   0 7496 3454 5 (pbk)
Flying Bombs – Wartime Bomb Disposal
0 7496 3210 0 (hbk)   0 7496 3453 7 (pbk)
12,000 Miles From Home – Sent to Australia
0 7496 3370 0 (hbk)   0 7496 3542 8 (pbk)